W9-BZP-036

The Kidnapped Kitten

Pet Rescue Adventures:

Also by Holly Webb:

Little Puppy Lost

The Kidnapped Kitten

by Holly Webb
Illustrated by Sophy Williams

tiger tales

5 River Road, Suite 128, Wilton, CT 06897
Published in the United States 2019
Originally published in Great Britain 2014
by the Little Tiger Group
Text copyright © 2014 Holly Webb
Illustrations copyright © 2014 Sophy Williams
ISBN-13: 978-1-68010-434-9
ISBN-10: 1-68010-434-9
Printed in China
STP/1800/0218/1018
10 9 8 7 6 5 4 3 2 1

For more insight and activities, visit us at www.tigertalesbooks.com

Contents

For Lizzie

Chapter One
Exciting News

"Laura! Laura!" Tia waved, as she rushed down their street on the way home from school.

Her neighbor stood up and waved back. Laura was planting something in her front yard, and her beautiful cat, Charlie, was sitting next to her, staring suspiciously at the turned-over earth.

Tia ran up and leaned over the wall,

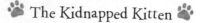

and her little sister, Christy, followed, panting, "You went too fast for me!"

"I'm sorry," said Tia, taking her sister's hand. "Laura, guess what?"

Laura smiled. "What? Something good, it sounds like."

Tia nodded. "The best. Mom and Dad say we can have a cat!"

Christy did a twirly dance. "A cat! A cat!" she sang.

"Oh, that's so exciting." Laura beamed at them. "You'll be wonderful cat owners. You were great when you came with your mom to feed Charlie while I was away. He looked pretty grumpy when I got back—I don't think I was paying as much attention to him as you two were." She looked up in surprise as Charlie suddenly pounced on the pile of earth. "Oh, Charlie! Stop it! You don't want it, you silly cat."

"What is it?" Tia tried to see what Charlie was batting at with his paw.

"A worm. No, don't eat it! Ugh!" Laura picked up Charlie and dusted the soil off his paws, and the worm made a quick getaway.

"He eats *worms*?" Christy peered over the wall at Charlie.

9

Laura grinned. "He eats everything. Especially things that wriggle. Bengals are like that. Really nosy."

"Charlie's a special breed of cat, then?" Tia asked thoughtfully. "I've never seen another cat that looks like him. He's like a leopard."

"Exactly." Laura nodded and put Charlie on top of the wall so the girls could admire him. He sat down with his tail wrapped around his paws and his nose in the air, posing. "Bengals are descendants of leopard cats—little wild cats that live in Asia. Leopard cats are spotted, like big leopards. But you can get Bengals with swirly stripes, too."

Tia reached out her hand to Charlie and made kissy noises at him.

Charlie gazed back at her. He had

his eyes half-closed, which made him look very snooty, but Tia thought it was actually because he was a little embarrassed about not being allowed to eat worms.

He eyed her thoughtfully for a few more seconds, then stood up and stepped delicately along the wall to allow her to pet him.

"You're the nicest cat ever," Tia told him. She glanced up at Laura. "You know, his fur's almost sparkly when you look at him in the sunshine."

"It's called glitter." Laura nodded. "A lot of Bengal cats have it." She rubbed Charlie's ears. "It's actually because some of his fur is see-through, but it looks like he's covered in gold dust. He's a precious boy."

"Hi, Laura! I hope the girls aren't bothering you." Tia and Christy's mom hurried up.

"No, it's fine. They were just telling me their exciting news." Laura smiled. "If you get a cat, then they can both sit in our front windows and stare at each other!"

Tia giggled, imagining it. Laura's

house was just across the street from theirs, so the two cats really would be able to see each other. Charlie liked to sit on the windowsill and look out. Tia always waved to him on her way past.

Tia ran her hand down Charlie's satiny back again. "Mom! Could we have a cat like Charlie?"

Her mom reached out to scratch Charlie under the chin. "I'm sorry, Tia, but I don't think so. Charlie's beautiful, but Bengals are very rare! We're going to get our cat from a rescue, and I don't think we'll find a Bengal.

"We'll probably go to the local animal rescue and see if they have any kittens available," Tia's mom explained to Laura. "Even though you are beautiful, aren't you?" She made coaxing noises at

Charlie, and he made his superior face again.

"Lucy got Mittens from the animal rescue. Lucy's my best friend from school," Tia put in. "She's got a really cute black-and-white cat, with little white mittens on the fronts of her paws. It's all right, though—Mittens isn't as beautiful as you," she added to Charlie, who was looking outraged. "Sometimes I think he understands everything we say," she told Laura.

"That's the thing with Bengals," Laura said. "They're very clever. A lot of them can do tricks, like opening doors— Charlie can do that. But it means they can be difficult to take care of. When they get bored, they can be naughty. I wouldn't be able to have Charlie if I didn't work at home. He'd be lonely if I was out all day."

"Cats need company," Tia's mom agreed. "But I only work afternoons, so we should be all right." Tia's mom worked part-time in the office at Tia and Christy's school. "Anyway, we should leave you in peace. Come on, girls."

"'Bye, Charlie." Tia gave him one last loving pet. "See you tomorrow on the way to school!"

"You don't mind that we might not be able to have a cat like Charlie?" her mom asked as she unlocked the front door.

Tia turned around and hugged her. "No! I just want a cat of our own, that's all. Maybe a black-and-white cat, like

Lucy's. Will we be able to choose from a lot of cats?"

"I'm not sure...," her mom said. "I'll have to call the animal rescue. Lucy's mom was telling me about Mittens, and I think she came from a lady who was fostering a few kittens in her house. I don't think the animal rescue is just one big building."

"That's probably nicer for the cats," Tia pointed out as she took off her shoes.

"When's our cat coming?" Christy asked. Christy was only four, and she didn't really understand about the time it took to do things.

16

"In a little while, I promise," Mom said, and Tia gave a little sigh of happiness. Hopefully they wouldn't have to wait too long....

"Tia! Tia!"

They were on their way to school, and Tia had been daydreaming about what kind of cat they might get. She jumped when Laura shouted after her.

Laura was at her front door, with Charlie weaving himself possessively around her ankles. "Oh, I'm glad I caught you! Is your mom around?"

"She's a little farther up the street, chasing after Christy," Tia explained.

"I don't want to make you late for

school, but I really wanted to let you know something...."

Tia stared at Laura, not really sure what she was talking about.

"I'm sorry! I'll start at the beginning. The lady who I got Charlie from called me last night—I'd sent her a photo of him, and she called to say thank you. And you'll never believe this, but she mentioned that she has a Bengal kitten that's ready to be adopted!"

"Really? A kitten like Charlie?" Tia stared at Laura, her eyes widening with excitement. "A Bengal kitten that we could adopt?"

Laura nodded—she seemed almost as excited as Tia was. "Yes! I thought of you as soon as she mentioned the kitten. The thing is, though, this kitten has a bent tail. She's still beautiful, but it's what's called a fault. It means she can't be in a cat show, and no one would want her to have kittens, as they might have bent tails, too. So I thought I'd tell you, just in case you want to go and see her. I expect a lot of people will want to adopt her—sometimes people wait a long time for a Bengal kitten. I wrote it all down for you." Laura darted back into the house and returned with a scrap of paper. "Here, give this to your mom. It's the lady's phone number."

Tia looked down at the piece of paper and read: *Exotic Cat Rescue,* it said, *Helen Mason*, and a phone number. But somehow, for Tia, the scribbly writing seemed to say, *Your very own kitten....*

Chapter Two
The Perfect Kitten

"Are we sure about getting a Bengal kitten?" Dad asked, looking at the Exotic Cat Rescue website. Tia had found it for him on his phone, so he could read it while he ate his toast. "It says here about them being *very individual characters*. That sounds like the kind of thing teachers say when they don't want to say *just plain naughty*."

Tia giggled. "Laura said Charlie's a little bit like that."

"Mmmm. But he's so friendly with you and Christy," Mom said. "Some cats aren't that friendly with children."

"Laura said Bengals can be naughty when they get bored and lonely," Tia added. "But Mom's around in the mornings, and we can play with the kitten after school."

"I suppose so," Dad agreed. "Well, there's no harm in going to see this kitten, anyway. What time did she say we should come over?"

"Anytime after 10." Mom looked at her watch. "We should probably get going, actually. It's about half an hour away."

Tia jumped up from the table, almost

tipping over her cereal bowl. Even though it was the weekend, she'd been up since six.

"Slow down," Dad chuckled.

"I'm sorry...," Tia said. "It's just so exciting!"

The car ride seemed to take a lot longer than half an hour. Tia was much too jittery to read a book or listen to music. They might actually be getting their kitten! She wriggled delightedly at the thought.

The house they pulled up to looked surprisingly ordinary—except for a small sign with a drawing of a cat on it. Somehow Tia had expected something different, although she wasn't quite sure what. She followed her mom and dad up the path, feeling oddly disappointed.

Then Christy clutched her arm. "Tia, look!" She was pointing at the window on one side of the front door.

The windowsill was lined with kittens. They were all sitting and watching the girls walk up the path, their ears pricked up curiously.

"So many of them!" Tia gasped. They seemed to be different ages, too—some of them were much bigger than others. There were spotted kittens like Charlie, a beautiful long-haired one with blue-gray fur, and a couple with creamy fur—*Siamese*, Tia thought. She tried to count them, but Dad had rung the doorbell, and the kittens heard it. They hurried to jump down from the windowsill—there had to be a chair or something underneath it, as they were all lining up to get down. Except that they didn't wait in line nicely—they were pushing and banging into each other.

Someone had answered the door, but Tia and Christy hardly noticed—they were too busy watching the kittens.

"If you come in, you'll be able to see

them even better!" A gray-haired lady looked around the door, smiling.

Tia blushed and hurried in, hauling Christy after her.

The door to the room with the window was closed, and Tia could hear squeaks and bumps from behind it. She stared at it hopefully, while Mom asked about the kitten Laura had mentioned.

The gray-haired lady—Helen, Tia remembered was her name—nodded. "She's a sweet thing—she'll be a very friendly pet." She beamed at the girls. "So, would you like to meet all of them?"

Tia just nodded; she couldn't even speak. Christy jumped up and down as Helen carefully opened the door.

"I have to open it slowly," she explained. "They get so excited about people visiting, and they *will* stand there just behind the door. I'll catch their paws if I'm not careful." She bent down as the door opened and scooped up a small kitten with golden-brown fur and the most beautiful leopard-like spots, who was making a run for it.

"There's always one," she told Tia, "and actually this is the little lady you've come to see."

Tia gasped as the kitten peered down at her. She had enormous round eyes, not green or yellow like most cats, but a soft, turquoise blue. Her ears were huge, too, and she had a long fan of white whiskers.

"Come on in, and we'll shut the door before they all try to escape," Helen said.

The room had been a dining room, Tia realized. It still had the table and chairs, but now there were soft, padded baskets, food bowls, and litter boxes everywhere.

"It's a kitten room," Christy cried, looking around. "There are so many!"

"Yes," Helen said. "And they're all looking for new homes."

"Oh…," Tia breathed. "And this kitten is old enough to come with us already?" She was still staring at the pretty dappled kitten in Helen's arms. "If she wants to, I mean," she added. Somehow it seemed clear that it wasn't only her decision. The blue-green eyes peering over Helen's arm were determined.

Helen nodded. "Why don't you try to pet her?" she said, lowering her arms a little to make it easier for Tia to reach the kitten.

Very gently, Tia held out her fingers, and the kitten sniffed them thoughtfully. Tia rubbed her hand over the kitten's silky head. "Oh, she's so soft. Like satin."

The kitten let out a mighty purr, a huge noise from something so small, and Tia burst out laughing. The kitten laid back her ears, her eyes getting even bigger, and Tia gulped. "I'm sorry! I didn't mean to scare you," she whispered. But the kitten purred again, and Helen slowly held her out to Tia.

"See if she'll let you hold her," she said quietly.

Tia glanced nervously at Mom. But Mom gave an encouraging smile. "She does seem to like you, Tia. You're so good at being gentle."

Tia carefully took the kitten from Helen. "Look at her beautiful spots,"

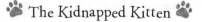

she whispered to Mom.

Dad and Christy were crouched down by the dining table looking at one of the smaller kittens, who was perched on a chair. "She's not quite like Charlie though, is she? Her spots are in rings. Like pawprints!"

"She is beautiful," Helen said. "You aren't worried about her tail, then?"

"Oh! I forgot." Tia peered around the little kitten, who was snuggling into the front of her top. It looked pretty much like a normal tail to her, only a little bit bent at the tip. "I love her tail," she said firmly. "It's so dark! Almost black, and the rest of her looks like—toffee!"

"She does," Mom nodded.

"So ... we can really have her?" Tia

asked hopefully. She giggled as the kitten hooked tiny claws into her top and started to climb up her shoulder and around her neck until she was standing with her front paws on one shoulder and her back paws on the other, like a furry scarf.

Mom glanced over at Dad, who nodded. "I think she's perfect."

The kitten purred in Tia's ear as though she agreed.

Tia had hoped they might be able to take the kitten home with them, but Mom and Dad said they needed to get everything ready first. Tia supposed they were right. They didn't even have a cat carrier. So after they'd finally coaxed Christy away from the beautiful kittens, they stopped at the pet store on the way home.

"Can we buy some toys, too?" Tia asked. "They had a lot of toys at Helen's house. I don't want the kitten to be bored at ours."

"What are the chances of that?" Dad laughed. "I don't think her paws are going to touch the floor."

"A couple of toys," Mom agreed. "But

we're not going crazy with them, Tia."

"I still have my birthday money from Grandma," Tia pointed out. "I could use that." She stood in front of the cat toys, looking at catnip fish, laser pointers, and jingly balls. What should she get? Tia could imagine the kitten loving them all.

She was just trying out a fuzzy mouse when a poster hanging at the end of the aisle caught her eye. It was for the local animal rescue, asking for donations to feed all the stray cats they took in. Tia looked at it thoughtfully. If her family had adopted a kitten from there, they would have made a donation....

She looked down at her basket and put back the feathery wand and the catnip monkey. She could make a bunch of feathers, and Mom had a lot of yarn. She would buy the mouse, but that was all. The rest of her money she dropped into the collection box. The bag the lady gave her to take home was very light, but Tia didn't mind.

Chapter Three
Milly's New Home

The kitten let out a despairing wail. She hated being closed in the cat carrier. It was too small and it smelled funny, and she seemed to have been in it forever. But then there was a clicking noise, and the door swung open.

The girl was looking in at her now, the one who had petted her and fussed over her. The kitten nosed forward cautiously. The girl rubbed her ears gently, and the kitten stepped out of the carrier and climbed onto her lap, which was beautifully still after the car ride. Then she peered around worriedly. This wasn't the place she knew, and there seemed to be an awful lot of people and movement and noise.

"She's so quiet," Tia said as Dad crouched next to her and petted the kitten.

"She's just not sure what's going on, poor little thing. She'll probably go and explore in a minute."

But the kitten didn't. She didn't go and try out the padded basket they'd bought, or drink from her new bowl, or chase after her fuzzy mouse. When Tia had to get up and have dinner, the kitten darted off her lap and hid around the side of the cat carrier. She didn't want to go back in it, but somehow it felt safe. She could have gone with the girl to the table, but there were too many people over there. *Safer to stay by the carrier*, she thought.

"I want her to play with me!" Christy wailed, pushing her plate away. "She sat on Tia for a long time! Why won't she play?"

"She will," Mom promised. "She just needs to get used to us, Christy."

"Anyway, we need to think about what to name her," Dad pointed out.

Tia peered at the cat carrier. She could see white whiskers sticking out around the corner of it. The kitten was so pretty, and she needed a pretty sort

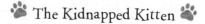

of name—like Rosie, or Coco—except that sounded too much like a poodle.

"What about Milly?" she suggested. "She looks like a Milly, I think."

"Milly…," Mom nodded. "I like it."

After dinner, Tia crouched down by the carrier. She didn't want to scare the kitten; she just wanted to show her that someone was there. The kitten peeked out at her every so often.

Tia had been sitting there for a good 20 minutes when Milly finally edged her way further out from behind the carrier. Tia held her breath. Would she come right out?

"Tia! Are you still there?" Mom asked, coming into the kitchen.

The kitten darted back behind the carrier with a flick of her tail.

"It's bedtime. Don't worry, Milly will be fine. Dad and I will keep checking on her."

Tia trailed upstairs reluctantly. It felt so mean to leave the little kitten all by herself. She lay in the dark listening to Christy breathing in the bottom bunk, too worried to sleep.

At least she thought she was. She woke suddenly from a dream that she couldn't really remember, except that it hadn't been good. She had been searching for something....

Tia sat up in bed. It was late. Mom and Dad had definitely gone to bed—

39

she couldn't hear their voices or the TV.

She could hear something, though. A sad, thin little wail. Yes, there it was again. The kitten!

Tia slid down her bunk bed ladder and padded as quietly as she could out onto the landing and down the stairs. She opened the kitchen door and whispered, "Here, kitty…. Milly…. It's so dark. I'll have to put the light on. Don't be surprised, okay?" She closed the door behind her and clicked on the light, blinking in the sudden glare. She'd expected to see the kitten dart back behind her carrier, or maybe she would be in her basket—but Tia couldn't see her anywhere.

"Milly?" she called softly, turning slowly in the middle of the room.

"Where are you?"

She has to be here, Tia told herself. *I heard her. She couldn't have gotten out of the cat flap.* Dad had put the cat flap in, but they had kept it locked—Milly wouldn't be allowed to go out until she'd had all her vaccinations. She was hiding, that was all. *Where would a kitten like to hide?* Tia wondered.

The tablecloth covering the kitchen table moved slightly, as though there was a draft—but all the windows were closed. Tia smiled and crouched down under the table.

There, in the dim light under the tablecloth, a pair of blue-green eyes shone out at her. Milly was sitting on a stool, with the tablecloth tucked around her like a little tent.

"Hello," Tia whispered.

The kitten stared back at her, and Tia settled herself against the leg of the table. "I'll sit here," she said sleepily. "Just to make sure you're okay."

She was half asleep when she felt little paws patting at her leg, and then Milly scrambled onto her lap and curled herself into a tiny ball.

"Tia! What are you doing under there?" Christy squeaked. "You weren't in your bed—I came to find you!"

Tia blinked. The light was still on, and the kitchen seemed very bright. "Is it morning?" she muttered.

"Yes! Did you sleep down here all night?"

"No.... I came down in the middle sometime. Owww, I'm all stiff." Tia tried to stretch out her legs without disturbing Milly, who was blinking at her.

Christy creeped under the table to join them and rubbed Milly's back, following the direction of the fur the way Tia had taught her. "I'm so glad she's ours," she said.

"I know," Tia agreed. "I can't wait

to tell Lucy all about her at school tomorrow."

"Oh, hello, you two—you three, I mean." Mom peered under the tablecloth. "Did you come down early to play with her?"

Tia gave Christy a look and nodded. It was better that Mom didn't know she'd been downstairs half the night....

After that first night, Milly settled in quickly. She didn't stay confined to the kitchen for long—she was much too nosy. She missed her old home and all her brothers and sisters, but now she had an entire house to explore. She explored it completely, too—every surface, every shelf, every cupboard. She wasn't big enough to climb the stairs at first, but whenever Tia and Christy were home, they were happy to carry her. And by the time she had been living with Tia's family for a month, she was big enough to scramble up them by herself.

Milly's favorite place was Tia and Christy's room. It was full of toys to chase and boxes to wriggle in and out of. She was also fascinated by the ladder to Tia's top bunk. Tia had carried her up there, but Milly wanted to be able to climb it on her own.

"What are you doing, kitten?" Tia said, laughing as she watched Milly from her desk. She was trying to do her homework, but Milly kept stealing her pencils and burying them under the bed.

Milly put her front paws on the first step—the ladder had flat, wide rungs, and it was easy enough to jump onto one. She managed to jump from the first step to the second. But then she wobbled and slid, and had to make a flying leap down onto Christy's bed instead. Then she went prowling off through the soft toys, pretending that was what she had meant to do all along.

Tia wished she could play with Milly, but she had to finish her homework first.

It wasn't until Christy came upstairs and let out a piercing shriek that Tia realized what Milly had been doing. One of Christy's favorite toys was a feathery owl that Dad had brought back for her from a work trip. It always sat propped up at the side of her bed because it was made up of a lot of tiny feathers, and it was a little fragile.

"Owly! She's eaten Owly!" Christy howled.

Milly sat in the middle of the bed, looking confused. Christy did burst out crying every so often; she'd gotten used to that now. But she was being very loud, and she was stomping around. Milly spat out a mouthful of the interesting feathers and slunk to the end of the bed, heading toward Tia.

"What's the matter?" Mom said,

rushing in. "Oh my goodness. Christy, I'm sorry, sweetheart."

"He's all eaten and ruined…," Christy sobbed.

"Tia, how on earth could you have let Milly do that?" Mom asked.

"I didn't see! I was doing my homework. I'm sorry, Christy…." Tia picked Milly up, looking guiltily at her little sister. "Maybe we can glue the feathers back on."

"You shouldn't cuddle her," Christy growled. "She's a bad cat!"

"Oh, no, she isn't! She didn't know."

Milly snuggled closer into Tia's school sweater, not liking the angry voices.

"You're scaring her!" Tia said, and Christy wailed again.

"I don't care! She broke Owly!"

"Take the cat downstairs, Tia," Mom snapped. "Honestly, after the pie yesterday, too. I never thought a kitten could be so much trouble."

"I wish we had a kitten that didn't eat things!" Christy gulped.

Tia hurried down the stairs with Milly in her arms. "You are silly," she muttered. "I love you climbing around and getting into everything, but the pie was a disaster."

Mom had been making a pie to take to a friend's house, and she'd left it out on the counter while she answered the door. She came back to find a very happy cat, and a lot less whipped cream on top of the pie. Mom had had to buy cookies instead, although Tia was sure it would have been all right

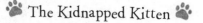

if Mom had just added some more whipped cream.

"I think you'd better try to be perfectly behaved for the next few days," she told Milly as she put her in her basket. "You're definitely not Mom or Christy's favorite cat right now."

"Do you think there's anything I can do about Milly?" Tia asked Laura, sipping her juice. It was the weekend, and she'd stopped over to get some advice on Milly's naughty tricks.

Laura shook her head slowly. "Not much. Just make her get down every time you see her somewhere she shouldn't be. A lot of it's simply that she's a kitten. She will get better as she gets older. Charlie used to knock things over all the time, but he doesn't do quite as much climbing now."

Tia sighed. It didn't look like there was an easy answer. "I guess I'm lucky she hasn't really spoiled anything of mine yet. Well, she did eat my sandwich yesterday while Mom was packing my lunch. But that's not the same as Owly. Christy is still really upset. She says we should take Milly back and get a better-behaved cat."

"I suppose the thing to do is make sure anything precious is put away," Laura said. "And shut the doors if there are rooms you don't want her in."

"Yes," Tia agreed. "It's just that Christy *never* shuts doors."

"Milly might learn to open them anyway. I wouldn't be surprised. Actually, Tia, I'm glad you came over," Laura said, reaching over to a pile of newspapers on one of the kitchen chairs. "I was going to talk to your mom or dad. Do you know if they've seen this?" She folded the newspaper over and showed a headline to Tia—CATNAPPERS STEAL PRECIOUS PETS.

"No!" Tia looked at it in horror. "Why are they stealing them?"

"To sell." Laura was frowning. "The thieves steal them and then sell them to make money. The thing is, this article specifically mentions Bengals. Probably because they're so unique. And I know that a friend of mine who has a Bengal

52

kitten caught someone trying to tempt her cat out of her yard. She doesn't live all that far from here."

Tia jumped up from the table. "I'm really sorry, Laura, but I have to go home. Milly's allowed out of her cat flap now. What if someone's trying to steal her this minute?"

Chapter Four
Trouble!

Laura tried to tell Tia that it was unlikely anyone would try to steal Milly, and she hadn't meant to scare her. She was still letting Charlie go out, but only when she was around to keep an eye on him. "Just to be safe," she explained.

Tia calmed down enough to finish her juice. But she refused a cookie, and as she hurried back home, she couldn't help keeping an eye out for cat thieves. *What would they look like, though?* she thought.

Tia went down the side of her house to the backyard. Milly loved it out there. She bounced in and out of the plants, and spied on the birdbath. Tia had noticed that only the bravest birds came to it now.

But Milly wasn't sitting underneath the birdbath, and she didn't come when Tia called, like she usually did. She was nowhere to be seen.

"Milly! Milly!" Tia called anxiously. She ran across the yard to look over the back fence into Mr. Jackson's yard. Milly liked it over there. Mr. Jackson had a goldfish pond. She

had climbed the fence at the side of the yard, too, but the people next door had a spaniel named Max, and he had barked at Milly so loudly that she'd jumped right back down again.

Just as Tia reached the back fence and looked through the trellis on the top, there was a splashing sound and a horrified yowl. Then something bounded across Mr. Jackson's yard. A small, bedraggled thing, trailing long streamers of green weeds.

"That cat of yours is after my goldfish!" Mr. Jackson shouted angrily to Tia. "Little menace!"

Milly jumped onto Mr. Jackson's garbage can and then up onto the fence, where Tia reached up and grabbed her. She shuddered at the clammy wet fur—

Milly was soaked.

"I'm really sorry!" Tia gasped to Mr. Jackson. "We'll keep her inside!"

"We'll have to," she whispered to Milly as she carried her across the yard. "Maybe we'd better lock the cat flap so you can only go out when one of us is with you. I know you won't like that, but I'm not going to let anyone steal you!"

Tia was right. Milly was not happy with being shut inside. She always followed Tia and Christy when they went out

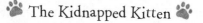

into the yard. She would chase the ball, and sometimes Tia carried her up onto their jungle gym. Christy had finally forgiven her for shredding Owly, and she would dance across the yard trailing pieces of string for Milly to pounce on. But sometimes Milly wanted to go outside on her own, too. It wasn't the same watching the birds from the kitchen windowsill.

Often she sat in the front window instead, especially in the afternoon, when she knew that Tia and Christy would soon be home. People sometimes pointed at her, and Milly could tell that they were saying nice things. One blond-haired man seemed to walk past the house often, just to see her. He always stopped and looked at her for a long time. And at the other cat, the one that lived across the street.

Milly liked to stare at the other cat, too. But he usually pretended not to see her.

"Look, Christy, Milly's watching for us again." Tia pointed to Milly, sitting in the front window, and Milly leaped for the back of the couch. She would jump from there to the arm, and then onto the floor to meet them at the front door.

"Nice cat!" There was a young man with blond hair walking slowly past their house on the way to his van. He was jingling the keys in his hand, and he smiled at Tia and Christy. "Is she yours? Does she always run and meet you like that?"

Tia smiled back. She loved it when people admired Milly. "Yes," she said proudly. "She's beautiful," the man said. "What is she, a Bengal?"

"Yes, she's four months old," Tia said.

The man smiled again and walked over to his blue van, which was parked farther up the road.

Mom hurried up behind them. "Who was that you were talking to?" she asked.

"Oh—well, he was asking about Milly," Tia said, frowning. She hadn't really thought about it, but the man was a stranger, of course. "He seemed nice...," she added.

"No, he wasn't," Christy said firmly. "*I* didn't like him."

"Oh, don't be silly, Christy," Tia muttered as Mom started to scold her for talking to people she didn't know.

"You were just coming, Mom. You were almost with us," Tia replied. But she had a horrible feeling now that Mom and Christy were right. She shouldn't have spoken to him. She sighed. "I guess we shouldn't tell people Milly is a Bengal, should we? In case someone tries to steal her."

Mom put an arm around her shoulder. "I'm sure that won't happen, Tia. But next time, just say that I'm the person to ask, and come and get me! Come on, let's get in the house. Milly's probably having a fit by now."

Tia had hoped that Milly would get used to staying inside, but the kitten still took every chance she could to sneak out. And she moved so fast that she was very good at it.

One lunchtime, when Mom was just heading out for work, Milly slipped around her legs, heading for the open door. But Mom swooped down and caught her just before she could escape.

"No, sweetie. I know you don't like staying inside, but it's to keep you safe." Mom sighed. "Hopefully the police will catch those awful cat thieves soon. It's been weeks. You stay there, and I'll be back later with Tia and Christy."

Angrily, Milly prowled back into the living room and jumped up onto the windowsill, watching Mom hurry away down the street. She hated it when they all went out. There was nothing to do. The cat on the other side of the street wasn't even sitting in his window for her to look at.

And she was hungry. She uncurled herself, jumped down, and wandered out into the kitchen to see if there was some food left in her bowl. There wasn't.

Milly stalked over to the cat flap and glared at it. She didn't understand why it didn't work anymore. It would let her back in from the yard, but now it wouldn't let her out. She pawed at it, just in case, but it still didn't work. It rattled, though, which was a good noise, so Milly pawed it again. This time, the cat flap shook, and Milly got a delicious whiff of fresh air as the flap opened inward a little bit. Then it shut again.

Milly stared at it. It had definitely been open just a little. She banged at it harder this time, and it flew open a little more. Enough for her to stick her paw in and stop it from clicking closed.

Purring with excitement, the kitten wriggled her other paw into the gap and then poked her nose in, too, flipping the cat flap all the way up so she could jump out. She stared back at it triumphantly as she stood on the doorstep, and then she pranced out into the yard.

It was sunny and warm, and everything smelled good. Milly padded across the patio, sniffing here and there, and glancing up at the birds that circled and twittered overhead.

It was the smell of the garbage cans that made her go down the side path. She was hungry, and although the smell wasn't quite right, there was definitely food in there somewhere. She padded curiously down the path and sniffed around the bottom of the cans. She was just considering trying to scramble up onto the top of one when the dog from next door, Max, came galloping across the yard on his side of the fence, barking loudly.

Milly shot down the path like a rocket, her tail fluffing up. She remembered Max, all big teeth and flying ears. She wasn't sure if he could get through the fence, but she wasn't going to wait around to find out. She bounded into the front yard and jumped up onto the wall. She then licked her paws furiously, swiping them over her ears. She felt hot and scared, and washing helped—a little.

The sun was warm, and slowly her tail smoothed down again. Milly's eyes half-closed as she watched the cars going past.

One of the cars stopped, a blue van that she was sure she had seen before. A young man with blond hair got out. Milly pricked up her ears. She had seen him before. He always stopped to admire her in the window. She pretended not to notice the man as he walked up the street, and she gave him a haughty look as he made friendly kissy noises at her.

But she couldn't hold out for long.

She padded gracefully down the wall to let the man rub her ears and tickle her under the chin.

Milly didn't even mind when he picked her up—she liked to be cuddled.

But then he locked his hand tightly around the scruff of her neck and hurried down the road with her. He opened the back of his blue van and stuffed her into a cat carrier.

And then he drove away while Milly howled and scratched and fought to get out.

Chapter Five
Missing!

"Oh! Milly isn't in the window," Tia said, sounding surprised.

"Maybe she heard Christy singing and went to the door already," Mom suggested. "I bet the entire street heard her."

But there was no kitten rubbing lovingly around their ankles when Mom opened the front door.

Tia hurried into the kitchen to see if Milly was waiting by her food bowl. There was no sign of her at all. "Where is she?" she asked anxiously. "Did you shut her in upstairs, Mom?"

"No…. She was definitely getting under my feet when I left," Mom said. "Unless she managed to shut herself in somewhere. Go and check, you two."

Tia and Christy raced upstairs, opening every door and calling frantically. Tia even looked in their closet.

"Milly won't be in there!" Christy told her, but Tia shook her head.

"You never know. Remember when she got shut in the kitchen cupboard?"

"She only went in there because that's where the bag of cat food is," Christy

70

pointed out.

But all the cupboards were empty, and they hurried back downstairs.

Mom was starting to get worried. "I've looked everywhere down here," she told them. "You didn't unlock the cat flap, did you?"

Tia shook her head, glancing at the cat flap. Then she frowned. "Hey, it's not closed all the way." She crouched down next to it. It was definitely open, just a little— the flap balanced against the frame. Tia gulped. "She got out."

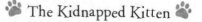

"But it was locked," Mom protested. "How could she have gotten out?"

"Look." Tia pointed. "It's still locked, but the lock's only a small piece of plastic, Mom. It keeps the door from opening out, but Milly's so clever, she didn't open it outward—she pulled it *in*. And then she squeezed under the flap."

Tia unlocked the back door and ran out into the yard. "Milly! Milly!" she called, hoping to see a toffee-gold kitten come darting through the grass. But all she heard was Max, whining next door.

"She's gone...," Tia whispered, her heart thumping so hard it almost hurt. "Someone's taken her." She knew that it was silly—Milly could be in Mr. Jackson's yard again, chasing the

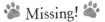

fish. Or messing around in that yard with all the berry bushes a few doors down. There was nothing to prove that she'd been catnapped. But somehow Tia knew. She just knew.

Milly peered out of the wire cage. The man had tipped her out of the carrier, and she had felt so dazed and dizzy after the car ride that she had simply curled up in the corner with her eyes shut. But now that she was feeling a little better, she was trying to understand where she was and what was happening.

Her cage was small—not all that much bigger than the carrier had been —and there was a tattered blanket in

73

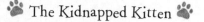

it, a litter box, and a water bowl. There was a food bowl, too, but it was empty. The cage was stacked on top of another one, and there were several more all around the shed. The entire place was grubby and cold, and it smelled like the litter boxes weren't cleaned often enough. It was dark, too—the only window was dirty and hardly let in any light.

But the strangest thing was that there were three other cats. Milly hadn't seen that many since she'd come to live with Tia and Christy. Occasionally she would see one of the neighborhood cats prowling through her yard, which she hated. But there wasn't a lot she could do about it, except scratch her paws on the window.

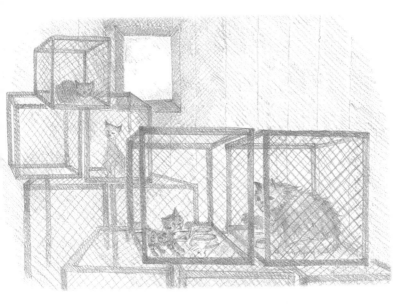

There was a cat in the cage right next to her, just on the other side of the wire. He was bigger than she was, and he had a large, squashed face and a lot of long fur in a strange blue-gray color. He hissed angrily at Milly, and she took a step back and almost fell over.

The big blue Persian hissed again and shot out a big paw, scraping it down the side of the wire with a screechy clatter.

Milly's tail fluffed up to twice its usual

size, and she hissed and spat back. She might be small, but she was angry. She had been stolen and stuffed in a box, and now she was stuck in here.

The Persian was still hissing but crawling backward now, his golden-orange eyes fixed on hers. They glared at each other, both of them refusing to back down.

As Milly watched him edge up against the side of his cage, she decided that there wasn't much point in continuing to fight. He was there and she was here, and neither of them could get out—that was what they should be worrying about.

She let out a last little growl and curled herself up on the blanket, wondering how she was going to get home to Tia.

"Anything?" Mom asked as Tia came in from the yard. She had been out to call for Milly again while Mom and Christy went to ask Mr. Jackson if he'd seen the kitten, and Max's owners, too. No one had seen her, though.

Tia rubbed her eyes, trying not to cry. She didn't want to scare Christy. "Do you think someone took her?" she whispered to Mom.

Mom hugged her. "No, Tia, I'm sure she's just out exploring. Don't worry."

But Tia *was* worried. Milly never went far. Whenever Tia called her, there'd always be a scratching on the other side of the fence, and a little whiskery golden face would appear over the top.

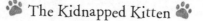

"Can we go and look up and down the street?" she begged.

They searched their street and the next couple of streets, calling for Milly and asking people if they'd seen her. And they kept going until it got too dark to see.

Mom said Milly would probably come back when she got hungry, but the kitten still hadn't returned by bedtime. Christy climbed the ladder to Tia's top bunk, and the sisters curled up together.

"She'll come back tomorrow, won't she?" Christy asked.

Tia tried to sound confident. "Oh, yes." *Please let it be true*, she thought. "We'll probably find her in her basket when we come down in the morning."

"She could be there now!" Christy

clutched at Tia's pajamas. "We should go downstairs and see!"

"No…. Not yet," Tia replied. She wasn't sure she could manage not to cry if they didn't find their beautiful kitten.

"I really miss her…," Christy said sleepily.

"Me, too," Tia sniffed. "But she'll be back tomorrow," she said, trying to convince herself.

Chapter Six
Searching for Milly

But the next morning, there was no Milly yowling for her breakfast. It seemed so unfair to have to go to school—all Tia wanted to do was search for Milly. It was Friday. Nothing important happened at school on Fridays.

As she trailed into the playground, her friend Lucy came running over.

"Hi, Tia! Hey, what's the matter?"

"Milly," Tia gulped, swallowing back tears. "She's disappeared. And I can't help thinking that someone has kidnapped her. Remember I told you about those cat thieves?"

Lucy's eyes widened. "Oh, no! How long has she been gone?"

"She wasn't there when we got home yesterday. She managed to get out of her cat flap even though it was locked."

Lucy frowned. "I don't think Mittens would ever do anything like that. What makes you think she's been stolen?"

Tia sighed. "It's just a feeling I have.... I know that sounds silly."

"No...," Lucy said thoughtfully. "I know what you mean. When Mittens was lost, I was sure she'd come back. She was gone for more than a week, and

Mom told me maybe I should give up, but I didn't."

"I forgot about that! It was during summer vacation, wasn't it? How did you find her?" Tia asked eagerly.

"We made a lot of posters and stuck them on lampposts, and I put flyers through the door of every house on our street, asking everyone to check their sheds. And that's where somebody found her! It was just lucky that it was a leaky shed and there was a puddle of water. Otherwise, Mittens would have died," Lucy recalled, her voice shaking a little.

"Posters...," Tia said thoughtfully. "And flyers. We'll make some tonight."

"What about this one?" Tia said to Dad, pointing to one of the photos of Milly on the screen.

"Mmmm." Dad nodded. "But she's more recognizable from the side, don't you think? Because of her spots."

"Look!" Christy said. "That's the one Mom took when Milly climbed into the cupboard!"

Tia enlarged the photo and smiled. Milly was peering out, looking worried. They'd actually moved the cat food to the top cupboard after her first cat-food raid. And Mom had even started keeping the food in a plastic container with a lid instead of a bag. But Milly was just too clever. She'd even managed to hook the lid open with her claws.

"She's so naughty…," Mom sighed.

"Mom!" Tia looked up at her. "Aren't you sad she's missing?"

"Of course I am, Tia! But she *is* naughty!"

"I suppose you wish we had a better-behaved cat instead!" Tia said, her voice choked with tears.

"I didn't mean that at all," Mom tried to say, but Tia was too upset to listen.

"You're glad she's gone!" she sobbed.

"Tia!" Mom snapped, her voice sharp

enough to jolt Tia out of her crying fit. "Sweetheart, that's just silly. Yes, I get angry with Milly when she's naughty, but she's a kitten! Kittens do silly things, and I know that. It's what we signed up for! Especially when we agreed to have a Bengal." She put her arm around Tia's shoulder. "Do you think you're the only one who read that book on Bengal cats?"

Tia gaped at her. She hadn't realized Mom had read the book, too.

"When I'm at home with her in the mornings, she follows me around, you know." Mom sniffed. "And I'm always having to rescue her from the washing machine. It's a wonder I've never actually put it on with her in it! I love her, too, Tia, and we will do our absolute best to find her."

"I'm sorry," Tia whispered. Somehow knowing that Mom was really missing Milly helped.

Dad smiled. "She's a little terror, isn't she? But nobody wants a better-behaved cat, Tia. We want *our* cat. Now I think this picture of her in the yard is the best. What should we say on the poster?"

Milly stared at the door, wondering when the man would come to bring their food. He'd fed them that morning, but the food hadn't been the same kind she had at home. She'd left it for a while, but then finally eaten it—she'd been too hungry not to.

She had tried to dart out of the
cage when the man put her food bowl
in, but he'd batted her away. She felt
hopeless—she couldn't see how she was
ever going to get out of here. And she
was hungry again.

Tia always fed her at about this time
of day. Where *was* Tia? Milly had been
hoping that Tia would come and take
her away from this horrible place.

She began to wail, over and over
again. The Persian
cat didn't join in;
he just stayed in
the corner of his
cage, sulking.
But the other
two cats started
to howl, too.

The door banged open, and the man stomped in, scowling. "Be quiet!" he yelled, hitting the front of the cage.

Milly let out a frightened little whimper. No one had ever shouted at her like that before. People had been angry or snapped, "Milly, no!" But this was different. She cowered at the back of the cage as he shoved in a fresh bowl of food. She didn't even think about trying to escape this time. She didn't want to get any closer to the man than she had to.

"I'm glad it's Saturday and we can be out looking for Milly," Tia said to Lucy. Her mom had texted Lucy's mom the night before to ask if Lucy could come and help.

"That's a great picture," Lucy said as she gave Tia some tape to stick the poster to a lamppost. "Anyone who sees Milly will definitely recognize her."

Tia sighed. "I don't think anyone will see her, though. I still think it was those catnappers Laura told me about. Mom did call the police, and they said they'd make a note of it, but there wasn't a lot to go on. Actually, do you mind if we run back and ask Mom if we can go and tell Laura what happened? I want to warn her to keep Charlie safe."

"Good idea," Lucy agreed. "If the catnappers did take Milly, I bet they saw Charlie, too. They might come back."

"Exactly." Tia shuddered.

They hurried back down the street to meet Tia's mom and Christy, who were doing the lampposts at that end. Mom had told the girls they could go farther up the street as long as they stayed where she could see them. Dad had gone to the street that ran behind theirs, just in case Milly had jumped over the back fence.

"Mom! Can we go and tell Laura what happened? I want to warn her to keep Charlie in."

"Oh, Tia.... I'm sure it has nothing to do with catnappers," Mom said, patting her shoulder. "Milly's just wandered off. Cats do that!"

"Please?"

"Well, okay. But don't bother Laura for long."

Tia and Lucy crossed the street and rang Laura's bell.

"Hello! I've just seen you from upstairs, putting up posters." Laura frowned. "Milly's not lost, is she?"

"Yes." Tia gulped. "Actually, I'm sure she's been stolen. There was a man asking me about her, just a couple of days ago...."

Laura gasped. "Young? Short blond hair? With a blue van?"

"I don't know about the van...," Tia started to say. "Wait, yes, there was a van...." She scowled to herself, wishing she could remember. It just hadn't seemed important at the time. "I think it was blue. You saw him, too?"

"Yes! He was asking me about Charlie. He was nice, said my cat looked very special, and I was all set to say Charlie was a Bengal. Then I remembered that newspaper article, and I just smiled at him and went inside. I felt a little guilty afterward. I was rude...."

"He was nice to me, too," Tia whispered sadly. "If he was asking about Charlie, that's not just chance, is it? He's a cat thief, and Milly really has been stolen." Tia's eyes filled with tears. "He'll try to sell her, and we'll never get her back!"

Chapter Seven
A Daring Escape

Milly flattened her ears. She could hear the man coming. She gave a small, nervous meow. He scared her.

He had a pile of food bowls in one hand, but in the other he was holding a cat carrier. What was happening? Then she suddenly realized—maybe he was going to take her home! She purred, hoping she was the one he had brought the carrier for.

She stood nicely as he opened the cage door and let him pick her up and put her in, although usually she would scratch and fight.

"Who's being a good girl," he muttered in the kind of voice that Tia would use. Milly still didn't like him, but at least he was carrying her carefully. She had expected him to put her back in the van. But instead, he put the carrier down indoors somewhere and left her.

What was happening? Why had he put her in the carrier if he wasn't going to take her home? Milly meowed worriedly, but she didn't howl like she had before. If she was noisy, she was sure the man would shout at her again.

At last, she heard him coming back.

He was talking to someone else, a woman, and his voice was soft.

"Yes, she's beautiful. Unfortunately, her owner couldn't keep her. The lady had to go into the hospital, so she asked me to find her a new home. She's very reasonably priced for a Bengal."

Milly tensed as he undid the clips on the front door of the carrier, and then he reached in and scooped her out. She did her best not to hiss, but she wanted to, and the fur rose up all along her back.

"Oh, dear, she doesn't look very happy." The woman frowned. "She's so pretty, though. Can I hold her?" And she took Milly, petting her softly.

The woman seemed nice—or, at least, a lot nicer than the man. Milly relaxed a little. She didn't know who this person was, but maybe she was going to take her back to Tia.

"Oh…." The lady ran her hand down Milly's tail. "There's something wrong with her tail."

"What?" The man's voice was angry again, and Milly flinched and pressed herself against the woman's coat.

"Look—it's bent over."

"Well, that doesn't matter, does it? I'm willing to sell her to you for a very reasonable price."

"I don't know. If there's something wrong with her...." The woman held Milly out to the man. "I hope I haven't wasted your time."

Milly looked up at her, realizing that she wasn't going to take her away from here, and let out a despairing yowl. The man snatched her and stuffed her into the carrier, slamming the wire door angrily. He looked furious—and the woman appeared very glad to be leaving.

Milly was worried that he might come back and shout at her again. But there was a loud bang, like a door shutting, and heavy footsteps went thudding away upstairs.

After a few minutes, she felt brave enough to come closer to the wire door and look out. The room was a kitchen, like Tia's, and the carrier seemed to be on a table. Milly pressed her nose up against the wire and then jumped back as it moved.

He hadn't shut the door! He had only slammed it—he hadn't twisted the clips to hold it in place! Milly nudged the door with her nose, harder and harder, and it swung open. She jumped out onto the table. She had to get away from here, as quickly as she could. She looked over at the back door, but there was no cat flap.

There was a window, though. Above the sink, like at home. And it was open, just a little.

Milly stood at the edge of the table, her back legs tensed, ready to spring. There were glasses and plates stacked by the sink, and if she banged into them, he might come. She had to be quiet as well as quick. She leaped right into the sink, and some knives and forks jingled under her paws. But there was no thunder of footsteps on the stairs. Hurriedly, she climbed up to the windowsill. She was free!

"What did the police say?" Tia asked. She'd been hovering by her mom the entire time she'd been on the phone.

"Well, this time they did seem to take it a little more seriously. They said they'd pass on all the information."

"They think Milly *was* stolen, then?" Tia said, her voice eager. "They'll find her?"

Mom sighed. "Look, Tia, the police will do the best they can. But there isn't a lot to go on, is there?"

"I guess not." Tia sat down at the table, her legs feeling wobbly. Then she frowned. "If they don't have much to go on, we have to find them some more evidence, Mom! Lucy said we should put posters up in the shops near her. There's a newsstand with a bulletin board—she says a lot of people read the ads on it. Please!"

"All right. It's quite a walk, though. Dad took the car to drive around and look for Milly."

"I don't mind!" Tia assured her.

Mom sighed. "Have you printed out some more posters?"

Tia picked up a pile from the end of the table and waved them at her.

"Now, you two go to the newsstand, and I'll go and ask if I can put a poster up in the library," Mom said. She was sounding a little weary. Christy had whined most of the way, saying she was tired of walking. Tia had tried to explain that it was all because they were trying to find Milly, but when Christy was tired, she wasn't easy to persuade.

Tia walked up to the counter, and the young woman smiled at her. "Are you looking for some candy?" she asked.

Tia shook her head. "We came to ask if we could put this up on your bulletin board." She held out a poster. "It's our kitten. She's missing."

"Oh, no! Look at her. She's beautiful!"

Tia swallowed back tears. "We think she might have been stolen. There was an article about it in the paper."

"I remember. Is your cat one of those Bengals?"

"Yes. A man was hanging around asking about her, and one day we got back home from school and she was gone."

The woman nodded. "The board is over there. You can move a couple of the flyers around if you need space."

"Thank you very much!" Tia went over to the board while Christy eyed the candy hungrily. It was covered in flyers, some of them curling at the edges as though they'd been there forever.

Tia started to take down a few of them so she could make room for her poster. Most of them were ads for things people wanted to sell— lawn mowers and strollers. Then Tia stopped, staring at the card she'd just taken down.

Bengal cats for sale. Reasonably priced.

And there was a phone number.

"What's the matter?" the woman called to Tia. "You look like you've seen a ghost."

Tia walked back over to the counter. "You don't remember who put this up, do you?" she asked, not very hopefully.

The woman looked down at the card. "Oh, I see. You're thinking—"

"It could be them, couldn't it?" Tia gasped. She was desperate for a clue. Anything that might help them track Milly down.

The woman sniffed. "As it happens, I do know who put that up, and I wouldn't be surprised if he *was* a cat thief. He's rude. I wish he didn't come here, but he picks up his motorcycle magazine every week. Some special order."

Tia stared at her. "So—you have his address?" she whispered.

The woman looked uncomfortable. "Well, yes…. I mean, I shouldn't give it out. Just don't say I gave it to you, okay?" She pulled out a big folder and flipped through. "Here it is…. That's him. But wait—you can't go over there on your own! Where's your mom or dad?"

"It's all right," Tia said. "My mom is just at the library—I'll get her. Seventeen Spruce Street. Thanks!"

She grabbed Christy's hand and pulled her along the sidewalk. "I think we're about to get Milly back! We have to find Mom…. Come on!"

They raced up the steps to the library and shoved open the door. Mom was in line, and there were a lot of people in front of her. "I won't be too long, Tia," Mom said as Tia came up to her.

"But I found them!" Tia cried. "The catnappers!"

"What?" Mom stared at her, and some of the people in the line looked around curiously.

"There was an ad for Bengal cats for sale at the newsstand. It has to be them!

And I have the address."

"Oh, Tia, I know you're desperate to find Milly, but you're jumping to conclusions." Mom shook her head.

"Why won't you ever believe me?" Tia said furiously. "I'm going there now!" She turned and marched out, Christy scampering after her. She didn't even look back to see if Mom was following. She just had to find Milly.

Chapter Eight
A Lucky Break

Milly threaded her way through the overgrown front yard and squeezed under the rickety wooden gate. She darted a glance back to the house, but the man wasn't chasing her. Still, she wanted to get farther away. Then she would find Tia. She set off down the pavement, sniffing at the dandelions and the parked cars. It was when she reached the end of the street, where it met another, larger road, that she realized finding her home was going to be harder than she'd thought. She had expected to somehow know which way to go. But coming here in a van, she had lost her sense of direction.

She set off along one road, but it didn't feel good. Milly turned uncertainly and hurried back. The other way felt as though it led home.

Milly plodded on, trying to sense the right direction. 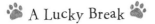 She wasn't used to walking so far, and the pavement was hard. Her paws hurt. Worst of all, she wasn't really sure she was getting any closer to Tia.

Wearily, she jumped up onto a low wall to rest. Another cat had scent-marked the yard beyond the wall, and Milly peered down nervously. The cat didn't seem to be around. She curled herself into a tense little ball and let her eyes close. She was so tired.

Suddenly, Milly's eyes shot open, and she almost fell off the wall. An orange-striped cat was in the yard below her, hissing furiously. His fur fluffed up so much that he looked four times as big as her.

Milly scrambled backward, her tail straight up, all the fur sticking out like a brush. She hissed at the cat, but he was much bigger than she was. Milly backed herself up to the end of the wall and then sprang down onto the pavement, racing away as fast as she could.

"It's this way," Tia panted, pulling Christy along behind her.

"We should wait for Mom!" Christy wailed. "I can't see her, Tia! We aren't supposed to go where we can't see Mom! We'll get in trouble!"

"I don't care! I'm going to find Milly. Look, this is Spruce Street!" Tia stopped, gasping for breath. What

if the man who took Milly saw her and Christy? He'd probably recognize them. "Be like spies, okay? We don't want the catnappers to catch us."

Tia pulled Christy in close to the wall and they began to creep along, looking for number 17.

"This is it," Tia whispered, a little way up the street. "Oh! The van!" She squeezed Christy's hand and pointed. "Laura saw a blue van when the man was asking about Charlie."

"Tia!" Mom was running up the street after them, looking furious. "How could you run off like that? You crossed streets! You know you're not allowed to do that!"

"Mom, look!" Tia grabbed her arm, towing her toward the van. "Look! It's the catnappers!"

Mom frowned. "Oh.... Is that the van Laura talked about?"

"Yes! And this is the street where the man who put up that ad lives. It has to be him, right?"

Mom nodded slowly. "All right. Don't you dare go in there, Tia! I'm going to call that number the police gave me. It's starting to look as though you're right."

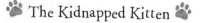

"Take a look at these." The policewoman held out her cell phone, and Tia stared at it eagerly. It had been so hard to wait for news. Tia had wanted to stay outside the house on Spruce Street, but Mom had said they'd better go home. They didn't want to get in the way when the police came.

"We might make that man suspicious if we're hanging around," she had pointed out to Tia. "We don't want him moving the cats."

Tia knew she was right, but she hated to walk away when she was so sure that Milly was somewhere in that house.

It had only been a few hours until a police car pulled up outside their house that evening, but it felt like Tia had been waiting for days.

"Is Milly one of these?" Officer Ryan flicked through the photos—a Persian, and what looked like another Bengal, but with a marbled, stripy coat, and another cat Tia didn't recognize.

"No…." Tia's voice shook. "Look, there's an empty cage next to this one. He's already sold her!"

Officer Ryan frowned. "Maybe. But he was definitely showing a spotted Bengal kitten to someone this morning. Another lady called us, saying that she'd been over there to see a kitten, and she suspected she might have been stolen. Maybe your Milly got out."

"Milly is very good at getting in and out of places," Mom agreed hopefully. "If any cat could, it would be her, wouldn't it, Tia...."

But Tia wasn't listening. She dashed away upstairs to her room and scrambled up her ladder to hide in her bed. She couldn't stand it. They were too late, and Milly was gone.

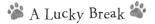

Milly kept walking all afternoon, even though she was so tired that she stumbled. The light was starting to fade now, and it was getting colder. Someone was walking along the street toward her with a dog, and Milly darted under a parked car to hide.

Even when the dog had gone by, she didn't want to move. At least under the car she was out of the wind, and she couldn't smell any other cats. She would just stay here for a little while, until she felt better. Milly dozed, her eyelids flickering and her paws twitching as the orange cat chased after her. It was chasing her farther and farther away from Tia....

She hissed and startled awake, not sure where she was. It was now bright daylight, she realized, as she peered out from under the parked car. She must have slept there all night, worn out from her long walk.

She stepped cautiously out onto the pavement and stretched. Then she heard voices. Children's voices. Not Tia and Christy, she was pretty sure, but still ... she would just go and see. Somehow she felt much more hopeful today, with the bright sunshine warming her fur.

It was a playground, and two little boys were chasing each other around and around. Milly paused at the gate, ready to run.

"Ooooh, look! Mom, look! A kitten!" The older boy dashed over.

Milly squeaked—she was nervous after the way that nice man had turned out not to be nice after all. She shot underneath the slide and hid there, shivering.

"Oh, Andy, you scared her. She doesn't know you like Whiskers does. No, don't try and pull her out, Billy. She'll come out if she wants to."

The woman's voice was gentle, and the fur began to lay down flat on Milly's back again. "She is pretty.... Oh!"

"What, Mom?"

"I think she's the kitten on those posters! You know, we said it was sad that she was lost. Her name is Milly, if she is that missing kitten."

"And we found her!"

"No, I found her! I saw her first!"

"Shhh! You'll scare her away. We need to call the number and say she's found. You two watch her, and I'll run and see if I can find a poster. I think I saw one on that lamppost by the gate."

Milly huddled under the slide with two curious little faces staring in. She was feeling a little better now—the bigger boy had surprised her, that was all. She sniffed at his fingers as he held them out hopefully, and he beamed and patted her head.

"Hello, Milly…."

Milly came out from under the slide a little more. The boy knew her name! She nuzzled his fingers, and he giggled.

"Me, too! Me, too!" the smaller

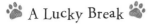

one squeaked, so she rubbed her head against his jeans.

The boys' mother hurried back over. "Good boys.... I'm just calling her owners now...," she said, crouching down beside them. She smiled at Milly as she punched in the number. "I bet you want to go home, don't you?"

"Tia, honey, wake up."

Tia blinked and rubbed at her sticky eyes. They were sore, and she couldn't remember why. And then all at once she did remember, and she gave a horrified little gasp.

Mom was standing at the bottom of the bunk bed ladder with Christy next to her. "Tia, why don't you get up and take a shower and get dressed? You fell asleep in your clothes last night!"

Tia peered over the edge of her bed. "Milly could be anywhere, Mom. That man isn't telling the police anything. Officer Ryan said so. He just says he's taking care of the cats for a friend. He must have sold her. We're never going to get Milly back."

"Sweetie, Dad and I think Officer Ryan is right. The man was showing someone a kitten just like Milly yesterday morning. You *know* how sneaky Milly can be! She ran away from him, I'm sure. The police have arrested the man, so they'll be able to ask him more questions. Dad's gone to put more posters up around Spruce Street. Do you want to go out looking again after breakfast? Should we see if Lucy wants to come and help, too?"

Tia sniffed and nodded, and Mom reached up awkwardly to hug her around the ladder. "Oh, that's my phone. Maybe it's Dad." She dug it out of her pocket. "Hello?" She listened for a moment and then she gasped, shaking Tia's shoulder.

"Someone's found her! She *must* have escaped! She's not even that far away." Mom put the phone back to her ear. "In the park between here and school. Oh, thank you so much! We'll be there in a few minutes. Tia, come back!"

But Tia had already jumped down the ladder, and Christy was racing after her.

Milly had stopped listening to the little boys as they told her how nice she was and what soft fur she had. She could hear something. A voice....

It was Christy! "Tia, wait for me!"

"Come on, Christy! This is where Milly is! They said on the phone."

Milly jumped right over the little

126

boy's knees and raced for the park gate.

"She's there! Look!" Christy squealed.

"Milly!" Tia crouched down and the kitten bounded up to her, purring delightedly. "Oh, we were so worried!" She stood up, cradling Milly in her arms like a baby.

"Thank you for calling us!" Tia said shyly to the woman with the two little boys.

The woman smiled. "I'm just glad we saw her. She's beautiful, isn't she?"

Tia smiled back. "She's the most beautiful kitten ever."

Christy danced around her sister. "We found you! Mom, look, here's Milly!"

"She's fine!" Tia called, as she turned to see Mom hurrying toward them.

"Better than fine," her mom said, gently tickling Milly under the chin. "You little darling—did you run away from that man? Hmm?"

"The most beautiful kitten ever *and* the smartest!" Tia sighed happily. It felt like she could breathe normally for the first time since Milly had disappeared. There had been a horrible lump of fear stuck in her throat all that time. "We got you back," she whispered, rubbing her cheek over the top of the kitten's head, and Milly purred so hard she shook all over.